ELLIS ISLAND
THEN AND NOW

by
Sharon Spencer and Dennis Toner

Lincoln Springs Press

Acknowledgements:

"Transients," "Despina" and "Sergei" originally appeared in *Crosscurrents, A Quarterly,* Westlake Village, Ca., "Literary Olympians" Issue, Summer, 1984.

An excerpt from "Oscar" and two photos were on the front and back covers of *Amelia* magazine, published in Bakersfield, Ca. in April, 1985.

"Looking, In, Looking Out," "Fatima" and "The Ones Who Stayed Behind" were first published in *Paintbrush, A Journal of Poetry, Translations and Letters,* Athens, Ga., Vols. XI and XII, 1984-1985.

"Dushitsa" was first published in *The Fessenden Review,* Menlo Park, Ca., Vol. 10, No. 5, Spring, 1986.

"Eight Who Stayed Behind" was published in *Anemone,* Chester, Vt., Vol. 3, No. 2, Fall/Winter, 1986.

The five photos in the "Suspects" sequence will be published in *Crazyquilt Literary Quarterly,* San Diego, Ca., Spring, 1987. *The Mill Street Forward,* Paterson, N.J., will print photos and text in its first issue, Spring, 1987.

Library of Congress Cataloging-in-Publication Data

```
Spencer, Sharon.
  Ellis Island, then and now.

  Includes index.
  1. Ellis Island Imigration Station (New York,
N.Y.)--Fiction.  2. United States--Emigration and
immigration--Fiction.  3. Ellis Island Immigration
Station (New York, N.Y.)--Pictorial works.  I. Toner,
Dennis.  II. Title.
PS3569.P457E45  1988       813'.54        87-26270
ISBN 0-9617589-3-7
```

Lincoln Springs Press

P.O. Box 269
Franklin Lakes, NJ 07417

A Collection of Original Stories by

Sharon Spencer

and Photographs by Dennis Toner

Contents

INTRODUCTION

During the first quarter of the century immigrants entering the United States from Europe and the Caribbean were examined in an enormous room in a massive red brick building on a small island located between New York and New Jersey. Today it is called "Ellis Island." Half of us Americans of predominantly European ancestry are descendants of at least one person who was processed in this room by Immigration Inspectors.

The newcomers had to prove that they were in good physical and mental health, that they were capable of earning a living and that they were neither prostitutes nor anarchists. Many people—it isn't known exactly how many—were unable to prove these things. Refused entry, they were forced to endure the return voyage by steamship. This meant a second period of eight weeks in steerage, the dirty, badly ventilated and often dangerous part of the ship below the water line. Many immigrants died on the journey to the new world. No one knows exactly how many perished.

Besides the people who were turned away were those who were detained, usually because they were afflicted with mental handicaps or contagious diseases like trachoma, tuberculosis or syphilis. They were quarantined on Ellis Island for a time, then either permitted to enter the United States or forced to return to their countries of origin—that is, if they did not die on Ellis Island.

Today Ellis Island has been abandoned by the government. Technically, it is "surplus property," up for sale. The only inhabitants are birds, primarily seagulls, and about two hundred thousand Norwegian rats.

"Ellis Island Then and Now" is an outgrowth of the photography project created by Professor Klaus Schnitzer at Montclair State College in Upper Montclair, New Jersey. Called "Ellis Island—Documentation/Interpretation," this is an ongoing course taking place at the abadoned immigration facility. Dennis Toner was a Visiting Artist associated with this project, and in October of 1983 he and I obtained permission to explore the dilapidated structures called "Buildings Two and Three." (Building One, which contains the Great Reception Hall, has been partially restored and is open to the public.) Buildings Two and Three are skeletons littered with chunks of fallen plaster and flaking paint. To us they felt haunted. They seemed to be inhabited by the spirits of the people who were once there, who, if they were fortunate, were held only for four or five hours. At times we thought we could hear the disembodied voices of our collective ancestors. We felt inspired, even compelled, to incarnate these voices in images. Dennis began the project of photographing Ellis Island "Now." Musing upon his visual images, I let my imagination roam in an effort to populate the abandoned buildings with some of the people who might have been at Ellis Island "Then."

Sharon Spencer

ELLIS ISLAND
THEN AND NOW

**sharon spencer
&
dennis toner**

"Dolores, just have a look at this room, will you! Just look!"

"Some sight, Concetta. Now what'd this place look like, d'you think, when our folks came through here?"

Dolores makes a face of disgust, then snaps: "Who knows! Look, there's flaking plaster everywhere. Just look!"

"I am looking. Yeah, you know, my Aunt Rose loves to talk about the days when she was....What's the word they use?"

" 'Processed,' Concetta. It's like what they do to cheese."

The two women laugh, then suddenly freeze. A young black man wearing a yellow slicker and dragging a vinyl garbage bag has appeared, silently entering the room the women have been exploring.

"Just me, ladies. I'm the Park Service man." He lets the earphones of his walkman drop around his neck. "Has either of you ladies got a match?"

"Sure, Hon. Here you go." Concetta hands him a pack of matches.

"Where're you ladies from?" Buster lights his cigarette.

"Me? I'm from Lodi, New Jersey."

"And me? I'm from Garfield, New Jersey. Where're you from?"

"Jersey City. Before that, Africa, Ladies. West Africa. What I meant was, where're you folks from in the beginning?"

"Oh, you mean, where are we from in Italy."

Buster grins, puffs on his cigarette. "Yeah, that's what I mean."

"Well, I'm not really from Italy," Concetta replies, tossing her head. "I'm from Sicily. Caltagirone, Sicily."

Buster nods. "And you?"

"You're a nosey young fellow, aren't you?"

"Yeah. There's not much happening here."

"Me. I'm from Chioggia. It's north of Ravenna. The best food in all of Italy is cooked in Chioggia."

Buster laughs. "Well, I just thought you ladies might want to know there's two hundred thousand rats here."

"Rats!" shriek Connie and Dolores in unison.

"They're Norwegian rats."

"Does that make a difference? I mean, are they cleaner than other rats? Smarter? Or something?"

"Naw, but they're better swimmers. How'd you think they got here in the first place?"

Dolores and Concetta shake their heads. Concetta exclaims: "I mean, this is a disgrace. The government letting our history rot this way!"

"Mine too," Buster says, eyeing the women as he nods, places his earphones back on his head and walks away, dragging the garbage bag.

"Rot!" Dolores snaps.
"Peeling paint."
"Flaking plaster. Everywhere."
"Pigeon shit all over the place."
"Broken down furniture."
"Rubbish everywhere."
"And two hundred thousand rats."
"Concetta, Norwegian rats. Remember that."

DESPINA

Sunlight and sea...sunshine and water, bright gold, bright blue...white houses...everywhere water and sunlight...

"What is your name?"

Despina gave a start. She was standing in a huge room partitioned into tiny cubicles by movable iron railings. The room was filled with women wearing their best dresses and big hats—some with swooping feathers—and men wearing the black suits they had brought with them from the countries they had left behind on the other side of the ocean.

"Where are you going?" The interpreter was only a few years older than she was and he had curly black hair and black eyes accented by thick straight eyebrows.

"Have you ever been in an almshouse?" he asked.

Despina wondered where he came from in Greece, but she didn't dare ask, not now while she was being examined to see whether she was fit to go ashore and live with the Americans.

Sun, she wondered. Where was the sun in America? The interpreter was very handsome.

A man came over, lifted up her eyes with a buttonhook, and squinted into them. Then he listened to her heart. Someone else tapped her back and made her open her mouth so he could look inside it. Then a woman patted her waist and stomach, feeling for a baby on the way.

Despina was angry. She had to squeeze back tears. She thought the handsome interpreter gave her a warning look. Keep quiet, that's what she thought his look meant.

Despina was being married in America. A man had written to her father on the island of Tinos and made an offer for her and now Despina was going to take a train to Cincinnati where she would be married to Dino Kyrtsis who sold popcorn that he cooked himself in a red wagon that was pulled by a black and white horse. She had seen a picture of her future husband standing beside the wagon. On the back he had written that it was red.

Dino Kyrtsis wrote Despina's father that he thought he might soon have enough money to buy a concession at an amusement park. Despina didn't really understand what an amusement park was, but when she got off the cold dirty train in Cincinnati, she found out soon enough. She was thrilled by everything in the park, but especially by the roller coaster. It was called the "Cyclone." There was nothing like it on Tinos. Despina loved it.

Dino Kyrtsis was nearing fifty and had practically no hair and Despina was sixteen and had a cloud of black ringlets, but he was good-natured and generous. Despina learned to like him, and when he wanted to have sex with her at night, she would create mind pictures of the handsome interpreter who had silently helped her answer the questions she was asked when she came to America. Throughout twenty-seven years of life with Dino, Despina remained mentally faithful to the interpreter, and he remained as young and as manly as he looked on the day Despina was pronounced fit to go ashore and become an American.

TINA

Tina rolled onto her side, pulling her shawl over her head to shut out the noise and the stench. Four showers for the men, four for the women, everyone stinking of stale urine, or of the herring that was all most people had to eat. The smart ones, or the ones who'd been advised by the relatives who'd preceded them, brought hams and sausages with them. That way they had something fit to eat.

She sighed, rested her cheek against her cupped palms and summoned memories of the hot baths her mother had given her every other night back home in Udine. There was a special pale pink scented soap her mother kept just for her, never allowing the other children to use it. Her mother knew how sensitive Tina was to smells and how sick she could become when she had to pass by rotting baskets of tomatoes or pears at the market.

Imagining her body lapped by the warm water, her mother's hands rubbing the perfumed soap onto her throat and shoulders, rubbing her with a cloth that was just slightly rough, Tina fell into a deep sleep, lulled by the motion of the steamship that was carrying her to America—along with hundreds of other Italians from near Venice; *Veneti,* they were called. At Ellis Island, she had been told, there were large showers with plenty of hot water. That made up a bit for the terror associated with the place. Because of their fear of being sent back, many of the people called Ellis "The Isle of Tears."

She fell asleep, dreaming of the warm soapy baths, smelling of roses, of the baths she would take every single night after she was settled with her father in San Francisco, California.

And soon—in her sleep—Tina saw herself running through the narrow streets of Udine carrying her father's mid-day meal to him in a wicker basket covered by a red napkin. He was in the big central piazza working with other masons who were building a new town hall. She adored her father and never minded being hugged by him, even when he was dirty from handling the trowel and the gritty cement. Tina's father, Antonio, had wavy light brown hair and large golden-green eyes.

To get to her father she had to pass a group of boys who were hanging around wasting time in front of the barbershop. They stared at her and called out phrases that were supposed to be compliments. Tina composed her face in a formal little smile and pretended she didn't hear them. She was fourteen and had already been in love with Giorgio for more than a year. After she had delivered her father's lunch and before she hurried back home to help her mother with the younger children, she would slip into the orchard at the edge of town and meet Giorgio among the apple trees. They would exchange kisses and promises to be true to each other for the rest of their lives.

When she got close to the group of working men, Tina ran faster. The red napkin her mother had tucked over her husband's food flew into the air and sailed off toward the open air cafe. One of the boys scrambled after it, snatched it up and returned it to Tina with a courtly gesture. He actually bowed low as he handed her the napkin.

Her father shouted a threat to the boy, but his tone was not really angry, and Tina laughed as she ran to her father. He swept her up, kissed the top of her head, and ruffled her hair, calling her "Carina."

Together, they walked away from the work site and sat down on a stone bench in the piazza. Antonio ate the loaf of bread, seasoned with oil and vinegar and covered with peppers and onions. There was a jar full of home-brewed red wine and for dessert, two juicy purple plums.

While her father ate, Tina looked around at the townspeople, the women balancing jars and bundles on top of their heads as they walked about with an air of proud indifference. The working men were sitting on the grass or lounging on their sides, unwrapping huge sandwiches similar to the one her mother had made for her father.

When he had finished his wine, Antonio said: "Hurry back home now and help your mother. Go quickly when you pass the boys—those sick calves—and don't give them the pleasure of even a quick glance."

There was warmth in his expression. Tina knew that he was proud of the attention she received from the boys. But even so, she has more sense than to tell him about Giorgio.

*****

She stretches, raising one arm above her head. Turning onto her side, she becomes vaguely aware of something...she moans...darting through the trees...their laughter...the sweet smell of the apple blossoms ...and she, lifting her arms and clasping her hands behind Giorgio's head, tugging gently at his hair.... Giorgio's hands moving softly over her breasts, caressing her nipples, her waist, her hips...smell of apple blossoms...that smell...so sweet....

In the dark steerage Tina opens her eyes. Next to her, having sneaked in among the women, a man crouches. His face is covered with dark stubble. His eyes are closed and he is panting; his mouth hangs open. Squatting beside her, he has thrust one hand under her skirts while with the other he rubs the swelling in his groin.

Tina sits up quickly and shoves away his hand, shouting: "You pig! You dirty pig! Get away from me!"

She stands up, pushes him in the chest and yells: "Get back to the men's side. That's where you're supposed to be. You slime!"

Now the other women are waking up and yelling at him too. Their shrieks wake the men, and soon one of the leaders, a man who is trusted by most of the women, comes to their side of the steerage. He grabs the molester by the shoulder and yanks him back across the space to the dark mass of sleeping bodies, the men.

Every night one of the young women or girls has this kind of experience. They cannot sleep with candles. It is too dangerous. And the ship's officers have refused to provide protection. They claim that it is too expensive to hire guards to make sure the sleeping women are not molested.

Tina sinks back into her sleeping space, crying a little. Actually, she is more angry than frightened. But she does not allow herself to sob, even though there are at least two more weeks to endure before they arrive in America.

TRANSIENTS

At this sink stood Karl Nielsen, eleven years old, born in Norway. When he arrived at Ellis Island Karl had two cracked ribs and a black eye. He loved a good fight and fought nearly every Saturday night later on when he settled in Ottumwa, Iowa. Here Karl worked forty-five years at the Morrell Meat Packing Company stuffing ground pork guts into sausage casings. One of Karl's sons became a Lutheran minister, Chaplain to the State Senate of Minnesota. The other son started a bakery which became famous for its jelly doughnuts. Karl Nielsen lived to be a hundred and two years old.

At this same sink stood Abraham Levay, who was born in Minsk, Poland, where his father was a bee-keeper and his mother a poultry farmer. A love of languages inspired Abraham Levay to add classical Greek and Latin to his mastery of Hebrew. In America Abraham Levay became a distinguished Professor of Ancient and Classical Languages at a famous university. His daughter Naomi was a successful screenwriter in Hollywood until she was charged with being a "Red" by Senator Joseph McCarthy. After that, she wrote sexy costume romances without any real sex in them; she did this under a phoney name. (This was before the time when such books, *with* sex in them, became best-sellers.) Naomi's editor found out who she really was. She told all the other editors in the trade, and then there were no more assignments for Naomi. Now she became a practical nurse, specializing in pediatrics.

Here, too, stood Vincent Scafidi. In Bari, Italy, where he loaded and unloaded ships, Vincent Scafidi enthusiastically helped his wife Maria create nine children. It soon became obvious that he couldn't support this family if he remained in Bari. Sadly, Vincent made the decision to go to America, making Maria one more "Mediterranean widow."

After he got settled in Elmwood Park, New Jersey, where he rented a room in the home of a distant cousin and worked as a hod carrier, Vincent Scafidi sent large money orders home every week tucked inside short affectionate letters. His heart remained faithful to Maria, even though his body was far from able to withstand the many temptations of the flesh that were available to a good-natured and good-looking man. Vincent always told his lady friends that he was married. The checks never stopped going across the ocean to Bari and the short affectionate letters never stopped either. Even after Maria died (Vincent was then fifty-four), he refused to consider remarrying.

After leaving Bari in 1921 Vincent never again saw his children, but he carried their pictures in his wallet and showed them to all of his friends, boasting of their health, strength and good looks. When Vincent died he was sixty-eight years old and still lived in a room in his cousin's house in Elmwood Park, New Jersey.

At this same sink stood Cosmo, "Buddy," Scocozzo. Born in a village near Sorrento on the Amalfi Coast, Buddy was amazingly good at many things. He could sing a Neapolitan ballad in a sumptuous and touching tenor while accompanying himself on the guitar. He could ride his motorcycle faster than anyone else around the steep curves and treacherous bends in the coastal road. He could lift heavier weights than any other man within fifteen kilometers of Naples. But the one thing he was the very best at was making smoked mozzarella.   No one in the whole south could make more irresistible smoked mozzarella than Buddy.

In America, where people were used to eating the yellow rubber the supermarkets called "mozzarella" Buddy "had it made," as people say in America. As long as he lived in a neighborhood where people knew the difference between the supermarket rubber and real succulent smoky soft pale golden mozzarella, Buddy could make all the money he needed to support his growing family of sons. Actually, Buddy hadn't even wanted to get rich in America; he had only wanted to avoid the poverty that was part of his childhood. People were always telling him how much like the Amalfi California was, so Buddy and his wife and his nearly grown sons relocated in the Napa Valley. Soon, they added making wine to making mozzarella, and they made so much money they themselves were staggered. Unfortunately, one of Buddy's sons was fatally attracted to gambling; he lost most of his share of the family business. But the others were much more careful. They went on making more and more and more money and having more and more and more children and still there was enough money to go around. Nearly all the descendants of Cosmo, "Buddy," Scocozzo were very happy in America.

LOOKING IN, LOOKING OUT

So this is America? A big deserted room. It must have been beautiful once, a palace. Ruins now. I wonder where the people are.

Ooooh, it's so damp out here! I shouldn't have wandered away from the group. Ivan thought I'd enjoy this visit so much. His treat. But I feel feverish. Chilled. It's so damp!

Where am I? Here, looking in. Yes, but where are the others? I shouldn't have gone off alone this way. Ivan is probably worried about me.

Oh look! There's Mamma. A big fireplace. Mamma, I can see you. "By the Fireplace"—"*U Kamina.*" Remember that lovely song? It's so cold out here in the garden! No, not cold. Damp. Of course, it's autumn. Wet, misty, cloudy. But you, Mamma, are inside sitting by the warm fire. "*U Kamina,* Mamma:

> Alone, you sit by the fireplace
> And watch the fire go out.
> At times the flames flare up
> But then they die down again.

Mamma, even though I'm here and you're there I can still see you. You're putting your head between your hands, rocking back and forth in your chair and silently cursing the letter carrier. He has brought you nothing, not even one card from your daughter, who's run away to America, leaving you to sit alone by the fireplace:

> Love is like the fireplace
> Where dreams turn to ashes
> And your heart is chilled.

Mamma, I feel like a ghost. There's nothing here in America. Nothing but this one big deserted room that was once grand, loved and cared for, just as I once loved and looked after you, Mamma.

Ooooh, the wind feels so cold! Weeds are growing inside the house now. Mamma, please speak to me! Say something. Just a word or two. Anything, Mamma, I feel so sick! So cold! So confused! I don't know if I can ever find my way back to you!

*****

"Darling, Katya," you wrote:

"I sit here by the fireplace writing to you. Through the window I watch the rain fall on the apple trees and, Darling, though I am inside by the fire, I can smell the apples and I can see your father as he was before the war. Imagine! We were married only eight months before he was killed! And you, Katya, eight months inside my belly, waiting to become the love, the only love that life brought me after I grew up.

"Forget the man who has left you, Dear Katya. You still think of him, I know, and you will always think of him. It is inevitable, now that you have decided to let his baby stay alive inside your belly. That man was ashamed of you, and he would be ashamed of your child too. So Katya Dear, it is better that you find for your child another father over there in America.

"Choose well, Darling."

"When I was your age, I didn't even suspect that life could be so long. For an old woman it is enough to sit by the fire in a small sod house and know that the garden will always grow enough for me to eat, enough to find even a small happiness in the smell of ripe apples and a song long remembered from the time years ago when I was loved by a man.

"Come inside, Katya, Darling. Come in and sit here beside me by the fireplace and we will listen together to the sound of the rain falling on the apple trees. And if you like, Katya Dear, we can sing 'U Kamina' together."

*****

Mamma's calling me! How can I get *inside* again? Oh, here's a stick. Maybe I can knock out some more panes of glass. I can climb through the window and go in where it's warm and safe. I'll just knock out one or two more. There! Now I can climb inside and sit by the fire. I will drink hot tea. I will rest against Mamma's knee. I will go to sleep, finally...sleep.

"Hey, Mother! What're you doing with that stick?"

Heavens! It's Ivan. He looks upset. "Oh, nothing. I just thought I'd...."

"Mother, what you're doing is called 'breaking and entering.' It's against the law."

"Oh Ivan, I'm sorry. I didn't mean to damage anything...anyone. I just wanted to climb inside where it's warm."

"That's all right, Mother. It's my fault. I shouldn't have let you wander off. Let's go back to the ferry dock now. The group's going over to Manhattan. Shall we have some coffee? Maybe you'd rather have tea."

"Oh Ivan, you're such a good boy! I'm so glad you're here! Tea. That sounds very nice now. Yes, I'd like to have some tea."

"Mother, you don't need that stick anymore."

"Oh no, of course I don't. Heavens! What was I doing with it in the first place?"

OSCAR

Oscar didn't really mind being held in a small room in the Contagious Disease Ward. He didn't really understand the name of the disease they said he had. He was so surprised at having a room all to himself he didn't even think much about being held here. They said he was very sick, but he didn't feel that bad. Maybe that was because it was so warm.

At home in Byske on the Gulf of Bothnia between Sweden and Finland he had to share a room with his whole family. There were seven altogether. Back home he had to take his bath in a metal tub which his mother filled with water warmed on the coal stove. But the water was never warm enough. In summer he soaped himself up in the water of the Gulf. The season didn't matter. Oscar was always cold. The Gulf was always cold—in every season. Oscar couldn't ever remember feeling warm enough.

Oscar fell in love with his room in the Contagious Disease Ward, especially with the white porcelain sink. It was the first one he had ever seen, and it was all his to use, all the time.

For hours he would stand in front of the sink and open the faucets, mixing the water until it became warm. Then, he would hold his hands in the flow and stand facing the bare wall, enjoying the warmth of the water as it poured over his wrists and fingers. Oscar adored the sink. He washed his entire body several times every day. Most of the time he felt warm and happy in his room, just a little too hot.

When the nurses tried to persuade him not to waste the water, he would smile dreamily and obediently turn off the taps.

When they went away he would go to the door and listen. After the nurse's footsteps faded away, Oscar would tiptoe back to the sink and turn the faucets back on so he could hold his hands under the flowing water.

After a few weeks—before the officials made a decision about whether to send him back to Sweden— Oscar died in the room where he had been happier by far than back home in Byske. He was fourteen years old.

THE ONES WHO STAYED BEHIND

When Buster walks through Building Three making rounds, checking for dead birds and other debris, he often stops and stands gazing through the broken windows across the strip of water, looking at Liberty Island where she stands, *the* lady, *our* lady, Lady of the Harbor. And at such times, especially on gloomy damp autumn afternoons like this one, he just closes his eyes. That's all he has to do to make the voices come alive. And here, at least in the rooms in the Contagious Disease Ward, the voices always question each other about the people they'd left behind on the other side of the ocean.

*****

"Hammid, who do *you* miss the most? Of the ones who stayed behind."

"That's easy to answer. Oh, Affifa! I loved her so! But I could not marry her. Affifa was a dancer. A Guedra dancer of the Goulimine. It's a sacred tradition among us. But—oh! It's useless to try to explain to people in this country. In Morocco a Guedra dancer is so loved, so respected that she'd never leave home!"

"And you, Angelo, is there someone you miss who stayed behind?"

"My sister Gina. She wore her black braids like a crown. When she was twelve Gina married a man from Controguerra. Up north. She went to live in a village near an old medieval fortress. Povera Gina! She would have loved America, especially all the white houses, the big American cars, and the shopping malls."

"Teddy, it's your turn now. Tell us all, was there someone *you* loved, someone *you* left behind?"

"Yes. Oh my yes! My older sister Nora. She was nine years older than me—babied me, you know. And I loved her. But Nora crossed the North Sea to Liverpool. She worked in a hospital—doing, I don't know what exactly. And she married a bloke from Cork. After that, I don't know. Nora stopped writing to us. I remember so clearly how she and I used to walk down the hill together to the town pump. Then we'd trudge back up the hill, sharing the weight of the bucket between us. Nora was a love—all right. Oh, I hope the guy she married is good to her."

"Magdalena, now it's your turn. Was there someone *you* cared for, someone who stayed behind, someone you still miss?"

" 'Lena.' That's my name. Please call me 'Lena.' Frankly, the village I come from was a bowl of dirt dumped on a rocky hill. Miserable, winter and summer, summer, winter, spring, fall, and all other times, it was a hell hole. The people were so beat down by the sun, they were mean. Everyone I loved died before I was thirteen years old. I don't miss no one from back there. I'll tell you, it was a shit hole, and I'm glad to be out of it. That's the truth. No one can understand who hasn't lived there. Starved there. Shivered there. A real shit hole." After a silence, the only response to her words, Lena says: "Now, Buster, it's your turn. You've been asking us who *we* miss. What about *you*?"

27

Buster shakes his head, fiddles with the buckles on his yellow slicker, and wonders how that tart Lena got the guts to turn around and ask *him* a question. After all, he's not from the other side.

He raises his hand and traces the bubbly glass, staring at the wet leaves pressed against the window. "Well, there's Aunt May. She married a man who beat her black and blue at least once a month, usually after he'd drunk up most of his pay. Aunt May had a son who was always in trouble with the cops. Her daughter married a steelworker...."

Buster breaks off, tugs at the end of the vinyl garbage bag in his hand, then continues murmuring: "So, Lena, all her life my Aunt May was a cleaning lady. In them days they didn't say 'housekeeper.' She cleaned office buildings in downtown Detroit. When Aunt May got old and retired, her daughter took her to Hawaii for a real vacation. It was Aunt May's first vacation. And do you know, Lena, can you guess what happened to Aunt May in Hawaii?"

"No, Buster, I've got a lousy imagination. You ought to know that. What happened?"

"In Hawaii Aunt May had a stroke and died."

Buster rubs his eyes with his fist. He jerks the vinyl bag several times and walks out of the Contagious Disease Ward, dragging the bag behind him.

Climb,
she said.
Climb all the way
to the top.
Everything you want
is yours
Just climb up there
and get it.
Climb, you weak
You, hungry, climb
Climb, you   sick
Climb, you exhausted
Climb,
You tortured newcomers
Just climb
and if that doesn't
get you where you
want to be
Claw
Claw, your way
to the top

(Everyone does it.)

SOFIA

From the window opposite her bed in the Contagious Disease Ward, Sofia could see the statue they called "The Lady of the Harbor." Usually, her figure was blurred, because Sofia was usually crying. When she wasn't crying or sleeping, Sofia stared at the silhouette of the Statue of Liberty and she prayed to Mary, the Mother of Jesus.

The immigration doctors accused her of knowing she had a contagious disease before she got her steerage ticket in the port of Naples. But it wasn't true. Sofia had never been sick at all until the boat was half-way across the ocean.

Her uncle had bought her ticket. He wanted to help her father, his brother, who had eleven children and a small scrap of land. The plan was for Sofia to work in America and to send money back home so that her younger brothers and sisters could come to America too.

The problem was, Sofia wasn't yet in America. Or was she? She didn't know. She prayed, her moist hands cupped around her rosary. Sofia prayed to Mary to make the disease that had broken out in her chest during the long journey just a heavy cold, nothing more serious.

Her face was wet. She felt hot and thirsty. She got out of bed and forced herself to walk across to the toilet which was in a corner with a screen around it. While she stood drinking water she looked at her face in the mirror above the sink. She surprised herself. She didn't look at all sick. Her cheeks were pink and her hair curled around her forehead in a new way. She had never looked so pretty when she was healthy.

She got back into bed and fell into a deep moist sleep. When she woke up a nurse was gently shaking her shoulder. A doctor came in. He bent over Sofia and listened to her breathing with an instrument he pressed to her chest. He stood up, whispered something to the nurse and walked out of Sofia's room.

Sofia fell asleep again. Three weeks later she died in her sleep. Her body was cremated in one of the furnaces in the big boiler room. Her iron bed was pushed through a machine that sterilized it with steam, and her contaminated bedding was sent to the laundry to be boiled.

Sofia Caputo was thirteen years old.

PASQUALE

"Detained!" Pasquale forced the syllables through clenched teeth.

"Detained!" Every day he stood leaning over the railing that encircled the top floor of the Detention Center at Ellis Island and stared down at the lower floors, cursing silently. *Porco dio!* It was the brother of that slut Regina who got him into this mess. *Putana!* It was her brother, the Judas who told the Immigration Inspectors about Pasquale's political activities back home in Comacchio. And now he was already in America, that pig Giorgio, while Pasquale was stuck on this island. It felt just like a prison. Maybe he was on Alcatraz and didn't know it.

"Detained!"

Regina *putana!* Like a fool he'd told people in Comacchio that he was going to America. Word like that travels fast in a place like Comacchio. Regina wanted to go to America too. So one night, one payday night, she'd waited for him in the shadows of the main piazza. A little drunk, he'd walked by and heard someone whisper his name, softly, so softly. He turned around and there she stood, leaning back against a pillar with one hand curved under her breast, the other stroking her plump thigh. Fool, he cursed himself, but could never curse himself enough. He had hurried, almost run into the shadows and fled with her into a dark side street. She had coaxed him inside a dark hallway, up a flight of stairs and into a small heavily perfumed room. She had lain back and raised her skirt. He had thrown himself on her, pronging her body with one or two rough thrusts. It was good enough for her, he told himself. It was what she deserved.

The next night he's having supper with his family. He's sitting at the table with his mother and father, his grandfather, grandmother and his three brothers when there's a knock at the door. In comes Don Lorenzo, the priest. On one side is Regina's father and, on the other, her older brother, that pig Giorgio.

Pasquale leaned over and spit down into the lower chasms of the building. Ellis Island! It might as well be Devil's Island. Or Alcatraz. Right now his wife—that whore—was probably fucking other guys behind the haystacks so she could make a bank roll to follow him to America.

And now he had a kid! For Christ's sake, a kid! *Pasqualino pico!*

As for Giorgio, Pasquale didn't waste much time cursing that son of the *putana vaca.* He knew he could find Giorgio later. He'd know how to deal with Giorgio when the time came. But there was Regina to worry about. With her kind of shamelessness she'd probably get what she wanted. She'd manage to save enough money scrubbing floors, or baking bread or even working in the fields, that is, when she couldn't get the village men to pay for it. Sooner or later, Pasquale was sure of it, sooner or later Regina would come to America.

Pasquale could see just how it would happen. One night he'd come home from work and that slut would be sitting on the steps of his boarding house holding the kid by the hand. "Here's your Pappa," she'd croon to the brat.

"Shit!" There was one thing that eased Pasquale's mind. In America at least he could get a divorce. You couldn't do that back home. Back there he'd be stuck with her for life. A divorce was the answer, all right. It'd serve her right.

All along Pasquale more or less knew that in a case like his, where there was no proof of anything, they'd probably eventually let him in. He had enough money on him to persuade one of the Immigration Inspectors to overlook his radical trade union activities in Comacchio. Pasquale was just waiting until he could be sure he'd picked the right inspector, the one who'd understand how important it was for him to get inside America, even just to divorce his wife—that whore.

DETAINED

In this room sat Lev Rominski who came from Odessa in the U.S.S.R. (formerly "Russia"). In Odessa Lev was a hat-maker, and this is what he was in America, too. Lev lived to be eighty-four leaving behind—as he put it—"four children and a daughter." All were healthy and all prospered in America, where life was much easier for them than it had been in Russia.

In this room sat Nina Orlovsky who came to America from the Carpathian Mountains. Discovered to be infected with syphilis, Nina was sent back to Tutrakan on the Romanian-Bulgarian border. There she married a horse dealer and spent the rest of her life marketing, cooking, sewing, washing, ironing and taking care of her eleven children.

In this room sat Rosemarie Moriarty who came from Cork in Ireland. In America, after she was released to a Catholic organization whose mission was to prevent unmarried women from becoming whores, Rosemarie became a lady's maid. She never got married. No one ever proposed to her. That was all right, because she thought of men as "dirty childish creatures," and the thought of being physically close to one of them frightened her. Rosemarie loved taking care of people, so when she had to retire to a home for old people, she was a great help to the nurses and nurses' aids. A quiet life helped Rosemarie live to age ninety.

In this room sat Anita Cuevas. She and her husband Juan left Bayonne in Spain because Juan owed money to lots of people. In America Juan and Anita settled near Santa Barbara in California. They had two children named Graciela and Jorge. Juan had many jobs, all for a short time. Anita got fed up with him. Taking the children with her, she crossed the border into Mexico where she became a flamenco dancer in a *cantina*. Soon after this, Juan was fatally stabbed during a Black Jack game in which he was accused of cheating.

DUSHITSA

"What happened to your back?" asks the Immigration Inspector?
"I was hit by a car."
"A car? In Karnobat, Bulgaria!"
"German tourists used to bring their cars."
"Okay. Go on."
"I was tending hogs. In Bulgaria I was a swineherd."

*****

One evening, just after the sun went down she had been walking along the road leading a pregnant sow. She was singing and thinking about supper—a plate of boiled beef with carrots and potatoes, horseradish, and bread. Maybe she'd have red wine too, and afterwards, a slice of white cheese.

The sow was tired. Grunting, she plopped down in the dirt. Dushitsa kneeled beside her and scratched her ears, urging the animal to get up and keep on walking so they could both get home to supper. Dushitsa was very hungry. She tugged at the sow's rope. Just as the animal gave a heave, shifting her weight onto her front legs, Dushitsa looked up and saw a car hurtling toward her in the dusk. She screamed and threw herself backward. Too late. She was struck and thrown into the air. But the sow had been hit first, and her huge pregnant body had protected Dushitsa.

She'd been lucky. Still, her back was broken. And it was crooked and had a big bump in it. It ached a lot, especially at night, but she had gotten used to that.

*****

"We don't need swineherds in America," states the Immigration Inspector. "Can you do anything else?"
"I can wash clothes," Dushitsa replies, full of confidence. "I wash clothes very good."
"Okay. We'll try you out."

*****

And so Dushitsa remained on Ellis Island as an employee. She had to prove that in spite of her crooked back, she could earn a living in America. She was assigned to work in the huge damp laundry room in the cellar of one of the big buildings.

It wasn't at all like washing clothes back home. In Bulgaria she'd always sung while she washed clothes. She'd take off her shoes and stockings, hitch her skirt up around her waist and wade into the water with the dirty clothes stuffed under her arm. She'd stand in the shallow water up to her knees and rub yellow soap on the clothes, then she'd bend down and slap them on the rocks. How clearly she could hear the slapping sound of the clothes against the flat stones of the riverbed!

Sometimes other women would come too, and they would sing together as they stood in the river, legs apart, singing, rubbing soap on the clothes as they sang a song that was just for washing clothes:

Gjura Beli Belo Platno.

Fast, they would sing in a fast tempo, their voices high and mournful but quick—punctuated with the shouts they gave now and then between bursts of melody:

Gjura Beli Belo Platno.

"Gjura was washing clothes," they'd sing, then shout. There was no sound to match the ripe voices of the women of Dushitsa's village.

It was entirely different, washing clothes in America. Here they had machines and big steamirons and rolling platforms that she pulled all around the place as she collected the dirty sheets and towels from the buildings at Ellis Island where the staff lived and where the sick people were quarantined until they either died or were sent back. Actually, a few lucky ones even recovered and were allowed to enter America.

Here in the laundry room no one sang except Dushitsa. She could always hear the high joyous voices of the women of her village as they sang, "Gjura was washing white clothes."

It sounded a lot better in her own language:

Gjura Beli Belo Platno.

A BEDTIME STORY

"I remember—I was ironing and my father was sitting in his big chair and—"

"Grandma, please! Not that old story about why you ran away from Hamah to come to America!"

"Why, Honey, are you already tired of that story?"

"Well...."

"When I was a young girl in Hamah—oh—about six or seven years older than you are now, one day I was ironing and my father was sitting in his big chair and my mother was sitting behind him in a small chair. That's the way it was in Syria, Honey. The men sat in the big chairs and the women sat in little chairs or on the floor. So, that day my father asked me if I wanted to get married. It seems that the father of—"

"I know, Grandma! It was the father of Ali."

"Yes, Ali. Well, at that moment my mother caught my eye and gave me a look that made me feel brave. So I said, 'No. I don't want to marry Ali.' "

"And then he asked you if you wanted to marry Ahmet."

"Yes, I was ironing, you see. Oh, you should have seen the iron. A great big heavy thing filled with coals from the stove. And I said, 'No. Father, I don't want to marry Ahmet *or* Ali.' "

"And then he asked you if you wanted to marry Yashar. And you said—"

"You see, Honey, I wanted to marry Sarosh. He was the shoeshine boy in the main square in Hamah. Sarosh was very handsome, and he always carried a big white box with bright red roses painted on it. Oh! And inside, there were all sorts of little bushes for putting on polish and shining the shoes. It was beautiful, Sarosh's shoeshine box. But I knew my father would never let me marry Sarosh, because he was only a shoeshine boy. So at that moment I decided to lose myself in the port and try to find some work to do so I could buy a passage to America."

"Grandma, tell me something. What'd you *do* to make the money to buy your ticket to America? You never tell about that part."

(Soft laughter) "Honey, you'd be surprised at all the things a young girl can do to make money. If she really wants to, that is."

"Grandma, what happened to Sarosh?"

"Oh Honey, I don't know. It was so long ago."

"Then why are you crying? You always cry when you talk about Sarosh."

"Honey, I loved him so much! Sarosh was so handsome. Not like the boys over here. Handsome in a different way."

"Don't cry, Grandma. Maybe there's some way you can find out about him. Maybe you can still marry him."

"It was just too long ago. It was a very long time ago. He's probably dead. But he had such a lovely shoeshine box! White—with big red roses all over it."

CONTAGIOUS DISEASE WARD
BUILDING THREE
ELLIS ISLAND

I never thought she'd look like this! So dark! Maybe it's just the late hour that makes her seem so black. Maybe tomorrow, if the sun shines, she'll brighten up some. Maybe....

I wouldn't have left Bundoran if there'd been any food to eat. I *had* to leave Bundoran. And now here I am, stuck in a ward with a lot of people who can't even speak English. No wonder the nurses talk to me so much! I can speak English at least. *Favus!* They say I have a disease of the scalp—me and these foreigners are "quarantined." *Favus!* I may even die here!

Now she's coming with the supper trays. " 'Well now, how are you boys this evening?' " That's what she said last night too. "Boys!"

"Well, Mr. Scanlon, here's your supper. Chicken, carrots and mashed potatoes with chicken gravy. See, doesn't it look delicious?"

"Nurse," I say, "How do you like living on this island with us prisoners?"

"You're not a 'prisoner,' Mr. Scanlon. And I don't live on this island. I live in Queens. Mr. Scanlon, you *know* you're not a prisoner. You're a 'detainee.' "

"I can't *leave,* can I? Just what do you think would happen if I tried to leave?" I give a snort and turn my head away.

She says: "Well now, you're not in a very good mood this evening, are you, Mr. Scanlon?"

"Neither would you be in a good mood if you were lying here staring at that big black statue!"

"Maybe you'd rather go back to Ireland, Mr. Scanlon. You can, you know. It's just a matter of getting the steamship company to agree to pay your return passage."

Go back to Bundoran ...to eat squirrels...sparrows.

"Maybe you'd *rather* go back to Ireland," she says.
God a'mighty!

MARINOS AND HELENA

Marinos was good at languages. He learned English quickly and was hired by the Immigration Service to translate during the inspection of Greek immigrants. While doing his work Marinos met many beautiful girls from Greece. He would stare into their large frightened eyes with such intensity that he sometimes forgot to translate their answers to the questions. It made him sad that the girls hid their long thick hair under flowered scarves. He wanted to look at the girls' hair, to imagine what it would feel like to bury his face in it and smell it.

When it was lunch time Marinos would carry a wooden chair to the side of the Island that faced The Lady of the Harbor, as people called her. There he would sit in the sun, staring at the gray water while he ate brown bread, feta cheese and black olives. Sitting there chewing and staring at the water, Marinos would dream about making love to the girls whose faint frightened-sounding words he translated.

His father, who was still in Greece, arranged for Marinos to marry a gorgeous woman who came with a generous dowry. Her name was Helena. Marinos wanted to live near warmer, bluer water, and so when Helena arrived, he quit his job as an interpreter and went to California with Helena.

In Los Angeles Marinos discovered that he was very good at making money. It was just a question of buying cheap and selling for the highest price he could get. Before long, Marinos was a wealthy man. He might have been happy except that Helena was very unhappy. She refused to learn English. She was afraid to go shopping. She complained constantly that she felt like a foreigner.

Beautiful Helena felt uncomfortable when people stared, admiring her strong features and vivid eyes. She said she felt "strange" at the supermarkets and other stores. Eventually, Helena's daughters started to go shopping for her and she stayed home, cooking and baking and reading Greek newspapers.

The years passed. Marinos was making more and more money and getting older and Helena was just getting older. It began to embarrass him to be seen in public with this dark anguished-looking woman who talked too loudly, always in vivacious Greek. People stared.

Marinos divorced Helena and sent her back to Greece with a generous settlement. In Piraeus where she was born, Helena bought a bakery near the harbor. She made all the breads and honey-soaked pastries herself. Now, no one stared at her when she spoke her own language, even loudly.

In Los Angeles Marinos went on making money. He had a lot of lady friends even though he was very fat. It certainly helped his popularity with women to be worth over a million dollars. His daughters fought with him, and after a while they stopped inviting him to dinner, even on religious holidays. Marinos didn't care. They were only daughters.

All his life Marinos felt guilty because it was so easy for him to make money. To ease his guilt he founded a charitable organization to aid poor Greeks in America. He tried to help kids who got in trouble with the law. One night when he was very old he was trying to give some advice to two runaway girls who were in a detention center. They were very tough girls. Marinos was old and no longer strong. The girls robbed him and beat him to death with bricks.

His daughters didn't even bother to write this news to Helena.

BETSKAYA

In the Jewish section of Zagorsk Betskaya was born and there she lived for several years. Her father and mother sold fruits and vegetables in front of their small house. During the days Betskaya played outdoors under their watchful eyes. It was always cold but also often sunny, and she felt more or less safe. Betskaya's nights were different, however. Then she lay rigid and terrified.

At night once or twice a week her mother and father's friends would gather in the front room. There was usually at least one person with a balalaika. They would sing at the top of their lungs. On these nights Betskaya would lie awake, wrapped in sheepskins, trembling nevertheless while she listened to the loud singing which was intended to muffle the metallic clicking of her father's printing press. He put out a newspaper that was confiscated by the Czar's police; that is, it was confiscated whenever they found copies of it. Sometimes there were brutal knocks at the door. Someone would answer. The silences that came then were even more terrifying than the loud music. After a while, the assembled friends would raise their voices again and sing louder and louder until her father had finished printing the paper. Even though the songs were chosen for their energy and the singers for the volume of their voices, they never completely muffled the clanks of the press.

When Betskaya's father had finished and the black ink on the papers had dried, the friends would hide them under their coats and slip away from the house.

One night when Betskaya was sleeping the Czar's police came and took Betskaya's father away with them. The next morning her mother fled to the countryside. The neighbors took care of Betskaya until her Aunt Sophia came, quickly bundled her up in scarves and blankets and took her away to a distant part of Zagorsk. Betskaya never saw her mother and father again.

To make sure that she would feel nothing, Betskaya refused to feel anything. For years she did not remember anything at all but arriving at Ellis Island. She was eleven years old; she was alone. After eight weeks at sea, her eyes were red and swollen.

"Trachoma," said the Immigration Inspector, pointing to the stairs.

Blinking, Betskaya followed an official upstairs to a small room which held a narrow bed, a bureau, a chair, and a sink. The hardest part of being detained was not to make her eyes worse by crying. After a few days her eyes cleared and Betskaya Zagorsk was pronounced fit to enter America.

In Dubuque, Iowa, where Betskaya was helped to settle by a Jewish organization, she got a job in a place that made jelly doughnuts. They were sealed inside little packages and sold in luncheonettes and at tobacco stands. All day long she stood in front of a white enamel trough and squirted red stuff inside balls of dough.

There were times when she tried to imagine what her life would be like if she had been able to stay in Zagorsk with her father and mother, living behind the fruit and vegetable stand printing a forbidden newspaper. Maybe it wasn't so bad to be terrified.

In Dubuque Betskaya's favorite weekend outing was to the art gallery. There was one painting in particular that fascinated her. She loved it. The painting showed an Indian chief seated on horseback. Wearing an elaborate feathered headdress, he was holding out both arms, palms upward, and gazing reverently at the blue sky overhead. Sometimes Betskaya would stand in front of this painting for as long as fifteen or twenty mintues.

After that she would meet some of the other girls who worked at the jelly doughnut factory. They would see a movie and have a soda or a banana split at the Greek's candy kitchen. Their hope was that some of the town's young men would drop in, and usually they were not disappointed.

BUSTER

That bird he'd seen upstairs was still warm. Buster shivered. It was always cold in the Great Hall and today it was raining. He was glad he'd worn his yellow slicker. He stared up at the tile ceiling. So dirty. The chandeliers were still beautiful though. Up above in the huge rooms where the enemy aliens used to be imprisoned there's a dead bird, waiting for him to pick it up and dump it in a garbage bag. Just thinking about its warm dead body makes him shiver.

He hears voices. A few tourists are wandering around the building.

"My mother got her name right here. Right here in this room."

"What was her name? Her *real* name, I mean?"

"Oh Rose, I don't know. It was Arabic. Something Arabic. But it meant 'lion.' So when the inspector asked my grandfather what his name meant and he said it meant 'lion,' they wrote down 'Lyons.' That's how an Arab got to be a WASP."

The women laugh. Buster smiles, thinking about his own name. His real name, the one his mother had given him, was Abraham Ezekiel Turner. He didn't like it so he changed it to Buster Turner.

"Rose, my grandfather changed his name to 'Miller.' Can you guess why?"

"Sure I can. There were too many Shlipkowskis in Wallington, New Jersey." They laugh again.

"Yeah. That was part of it. But there was something else too. In Yugoslavia we were called 'Chivarich.' You'll never guess what that means."

"No, Irene, I guess I won't guess what 'Chivarich' means."

" 'Pig's ass,' Rose. That's what 'Chivarich' means. You see when the Turks came to take the census way back sometime in some other century, my great great grandfather, or whatever, he told the Turks his name was 'pig's ass,' and that's what the idiots wrote down."

The women laugh again. They catch sight of Buster. Rose gives a start.

"Just me, ladies. I'm the Park Custodian." Buster chuckles. "Say, that was funny. About the name— 'pig's ass'."

There is a silence. Then Irene asks: "What's *your* name?"

"Buster Turner." He buckles up his slicker. It's nearly time for the ferry to come and take him back to Brooklyn.

"Is that your real name? I mean, we have made-up names."

"My 'real' name?" he echoes. "How would I know my 'real' name? My ancestors were slaves."

The women nod, say things like, "Of course. Yes. Naturally."

"You wouldn't catch me working here!" Irene says. "It's so lonely. So cold. Creepy!"

"Yeah," Buster replies with a nod. "Well, Ladies, I gotta go now. The ferry's coming." He walks out of the Great Hall, dragging a black vinyl garbage bag behind him.

FATIMA

There is a crash. The sound of glass shattering. A woman's voice, at first low, then a flow of words, high and sharp. The words stop. There is the sound of short regular screams, evenly paced, mechanical. A shrill calliope of terror. Two Immigration Inspectors are standing in a wide corridor filled with light.

"What's going on in there?" one asks, jerking his head toward the door marked WOMEN.

"Locked herself in. On the way over she went crazy. No one can control her. Not even her husband."

"Is that him?"

A man is walking up and down in the bay area in front of the large bright windows. He is young, dark, bearded. He is wearing a black suit. On his head is a white turban, around his throat a red and gold scarf. Head lowered, he walks up and down, clasping and unclasping his hands. He does not seem to notice the Immigration Inspectors.

A calliope of terror. The short sharp screams continue to pierce the morning. Then there is a heavy thud. A flow of words, high and sharp. A scream, prolonged.

The pacing man lifts his head, covers his face with his hands, groans.

"Who's handling this?" asks one of the inspectors.

"Allen. She's Allen's case."

"So it's back to Damascus for this one, right?"

The screams continue. Then a sustained flow of sharp words.

The pacing man stops, crouches, his elbows on his knees, face in cupped hands. He murmurs swift urgent-sounding words into his hands.

"What's he doing? Praying?"

"Beats me!"

Four men wearing white uniforms come hurrying down the corridor. One holds a ring of keys, another, a hypodermic needle.

The crouching husband throws them a swift glance.

"Say, did you see that woman before she locked herself in the restroom?"

"No."

"She was some sight! Tall and wild-looking. Wearing those white robes they like. Black and red scarves. Lots of jewelry. Looked like a real queen!"

"What'll he do if they send her back?"

"Who knows? He can go back with her. He can stay here. Or he can send home for another wife. Maybe he already has another wife. Those people do that, you know."

Dear James,

I'm working at Ellis Island nights, as a watchman. To keep kids from stealing what's left of the furniture. Who'd believe the place is a total ruin now, like me. Seventy, eighty years ago, this was a handsome place, good red brick buildings with fine gardens and a little park for the workers. Now I walk up and down the halls, listening to the rats. But it's a job. The nights are long, you know, when you've no one to talk to. So I walk up and down the halls. The place is full of rats, so I walk and I remember.

It was the old curse of Ulster, James, that's what made you and me quarrel. Macha's curse, as the old legend says. It's all gone wrong, you see. So here I am, walking and remembering.

D'you recall those mornings when we'd get up and tear through the wet grass to the outhouse? Rooster'd be crowing and we'd throw corn at him for fum. Mother'd be at the stove brewing the tea and burning the toast. Did you ever wonder why she always burned the toast, James, then threw it out for the birds and started again?

A brother is a friend not to be taken for granted. Macha's curse, sure, that's what caused our quarrel, and over politics too! Dirty politics! Over here I've never had a friend as good as you, James. Lord, I can smell the burned toast now! A kind of rage was in Mother some mornings. I could feel it, not just when she gave me a whipping either.

D'you recall the afternoon we buried ourselves in the leaves, James? We were supposed to be cleaning out the cow shed but instead we raked up a mountain of leaves and buried ourselves in it. She came out the backdoor waving a willow switch and yelling our names. We jumped out, screeching and waving our arms around, as if we could scare Mother. She just laughed and came after us,but she was laughing too hard to do us any harm.

I'll tell you, James, walking up and down these halls is a disastrous way to spend a night. Maybe it's my age, but I seem to think about home nearly all the time these days.

Big shot that I was, I had to come to America. Separate myself from the rest of you. So now I spend my nights walking up and down these big halls. They're full of leaves. And the place itself is just surplus government property, they say. The Americans were welcomed here, you see, at one time, but now the government wants to sell it to a hotel chain. What can I say? Surplus government property! It's the modern way of thinking.

James, d'you recall the winters, the fat snowflakes coming down slow and easy on the cow shed? And the way the frost silvered the milk bucket? The icicles hanging from the mailbox and how we figured out the perfect murder with an icicle dagger?

Sometimes, James, I think I gave up too much for life over here. And so now I walk through these halls, listening to the rats and remembering. This remembering has got to be like an activity now. It seems like a project with its own real importance, you see. The point of life now being lived backward.

SUSPECTS (I)

June 18, 1951
Oleg and I have been refused permission to enter the United States. We've been sent to an immigration detention center for "special" cases, Ellis Island where officials question Oleg repeatedly while they wait for information to arrive about his past in the Soviet Union before he emigrated to Brazil.

They led us past a huge room that must once have been elegant, once a ballroom or a theater, and there stood a ruined piano with a broken keyboard. I looked, and in an instant you were here with me, standing behind the piano, listening, nodding, keeping the rhythm as I played. We were always together in those days, always, always together every minute we could sneak from school or the social life that was forced on us.

SUSPECTS (II)

June 20, 1951
Several times a day we were led through the decaying halls of the buildings that are no longer used, on our way to the one building that still contains offices and personnel. There the officials go on questioning Oleg, asking him all sorts of things about the past. And he doesn't remember any longer. Oleg, so much older than I am! Father's choice, of course. To punish me.

Today as I passed by the room in which the abandoned piano stands, I stopped and looked. I took just one quick look, and I saw you standing there. I'm sure I saw you. There was a blur, a movement. I'm sure of it.

But then maybe it was only a shadow.

SUSPECTS (III)

June 23, 1951
They may make us go back to Brazil. It is the beginning and the end of my musical career in New York. In a day or so, say the officials, we will know whether the United States is willing to issue a visa to a man with Oleg's political past and to his wife, another suspect.

But then, why did I think I had to come to New York to have a career in music? Every few hours now I walk through the empty halls of this prison (for it is a prison) toward the room in which the ruined piano stands. And I stop there and look at it, my eyes moving up and down the broken keys. Always, when I do this I see your hands. I see your hands and I feel—

What pain! The day Father told you he would not allow you to study music but that I could if I wished.

And now I am so...so...oh! How can I express—

SUSPECTS (IV)

this love....too deep....so strong....now I begin to hope that we will have to return to Sao Paolo where you are waiting behind the piano where you have always waited to be with me behind the piano at the open window that looks onto the garden, scraps of plaster all over the floor. The past in ruins.

The officials have just told Oleg that we have a choice of returning to Brazil or entering the United States provisionally for one month.

Oh my love, do you know why Father made me marry Oleg? It was to separate us, that was why. People told him our love was unnatural and he decided to separate us forever. But nothing can do that.

Finally, this completeness is what I understand, and I gaze at the deserted room, at the wild foliage thrusting through the window and at you with eyes fully open, for I am more and more certain we are coming home again.

SUSPECTS (V)

Nothing can separate us. Nothing. Father should have known that. Whatever happens, we two will always be together, bound by the notes played by hands neither yours nor mine, our hands.

EIGHT WHO STAYED

One	Two
Three	Four
Five	Six
Seven	Eight

Number Seven
Koskoff, Emmanuel. Born, Poland. Streetcleaner in Lublin. Died of influenza at Ellis Island.

Number Three
Schwarzmann, Aristide. Born, Neubrandenburg, Germany. Until emigration, a hod carrier. Died of complications connected with typhus fever. Ellis Island.

Number Four
Lazzaro, Cettina. Born, Isole, Lipari, Italy. Until age seventeen, wife of Giuseppe. Died of complications connected with self-inflicted abortion. Ellis Island.

Number Five
Avallone, Vincenzo. Born, Canicatti, Italy. Age three, died of dysentery at Ellis Island.

One	Two
Three	Four
Five	Six
Seven	Eight

Number One
Lavroff, Ruth. Born, Voronezh, Soviet Union. Milliner until emigrating and dying of a stroke after disembarking and while being processed at Ellis Island.

Number Eight

Pinuccia Baletti. Wife of Tommaso and mother of Nina, Vittorio, Maria, Lisa, Giorgio and Angelo. Died at Ellis Island of causes undiagnosed.

Number Six

Assenheimer, Inge. Born, Dinkelsbuhl, Germany. Died, age eleven months of typhus fever at Ellis Island.

Number Two

Sciarrillo, Filippo. Born, Trapanti, Sicily. Customs inspector until his death at age forty-eight, Ellis Island.

One	Two
Three	Four
Five	Six
Seven	Eight
	Dead
	at
	Ellis
	Island

ONE NATION UNDER GOD

"Okay, kids, let's stop here for a few minutes. See, someone's draped the flag over an old abandoned trunk. At least, I think that's what it is. Now, let's all say the Pledge of Allegiance. All together now...."

"Good! That was fine! Now, can anyone tell me why we made this class trip to Ellis Island?"

"Sure. We came to see where our ancestors landed when they got here."

"Thanks, Billy. *All* Americans?"

"No, just the ones that came third class. 'Steerage,' it was called."

"That's right. Now, did any of your great grandparents come to America in the steerage of some ship?"

"Yeah. My great grandpa did. He said it was unfair."

"What was 'unfair,' Joshua?"

"Unfair, because the first and second class passengers didn't have to be examined here. They didn't have to come to Ellis Island at all. Is that fair? This is America—where everybody's supposed to be equal."

"Well, Joshua, your great grandfather has a point. But you see, a lot of the newcomers had—uh—lice and other contagious diseases. Lots of diseases were contagious in those days. The immigration officials didn't want people to bring those diseases into the country. Like trachoma, for example. Do any of you know what that is? Michael, are you raising your hand or just scratching your head?"

"I heard about that disease. It makes you go blind. Lots of Arabs have it. That's what my dad told me."

"I don't know about that but in the old days—"

"Mr. Stevens, this place is weird. It's not fixed up. Why did the government leave it like this, like a slum?"

"Well, Jean, it's not really a slum, you see, because people don't actually live here. I guess the government didn't need it anymore and didn't want to spend money fixing it up, so...."

"My mom told me about trachoma. When she saw me reading that book you assigned, she told me her grandmother's sister had to go back to Italy, because she had tra—trachoma. And my great grandfather had to go back too, because she was just a little kid, and someone had to go with her."

"A child might be too young to travel so far alone."

"Herring. That's all they had to eat. Herring and stale bread."

"Danny, where did you get that information?"

"From a book. My history teacher made us read some stuff about what it was like—coming here. It was called—"

"Danny, we don't need to know what it's called. People had to endure hardships when they came here. Our ancestors must have been very brave to make the journey to America."

"Not mine! All they had to do was go to the airport and get on a plane! It's so easy we go back to San Juan every summer. And we take a lot of presents to my cousins."

"Do they want to come to America too, Carlos?"

"No, Sir. It's too cold for them up here. They'd rather stay in Puerto Rico."

"Yeah. I know what you mean. Not everyone wants to come to America."

"I don't believe you. Everyone wants to come to America."

"Oh yeah? Let me tell you about my cousin Vladimir. He came over here from Yugoslavia. It was just a visit. His sister won a trip to New York when she bought a new washing machine. It was a drawing and she won. But she couldn't take the trip because of her kids, so she gave Vladimir her free trip. But after two days in New York he went back to Yugoslavia."

"Why was that, Sasha? Why did your cousin go back to Yugoslavia after two days in New York?"

"Well, see, he likes to eat good. And he said the air smelled so bad he lost his taste for food. So he went back home."

" 'Eat *well*,' Sasha. Well, people have different reasons for coming to America, don't they?"

"*Tell* me about it! *My* ancestors were ambushed, put in irons and tied up in the holds of slave ships. They were real brave. Otherwise, they be *dead*."

"A good point, Herbert. Afro-Americans didn't have any choice about coming to America."

"And lots went back to Africa too. Marcus Garvey led them back to form the state of Liberia."

"Yes, well, that's another story. You see, every family has its reasons for coming to America. Meenal, why did your family come to America?"

"Mr. Stevens, I don't *have* an Indian family. You know that. They were killed in a riot. Besides, I was one of those people that Gandhi called 'God's Children.' I have an adopted family. I'm happy in America. But I agree with Sasha's cousin about one thing. The air. It smells so bad, I feel sick when I breathe."

"I see. Yes...well...now, Class, we'd better be moving on. I want you to go inside this big building so you can see the Great Reception Hall where the newcomers were examined. Hurry up now! We don't have a lot of time. We want to save plenty of time for our visit to Liberty Island."